The Blade & Blaze Story: A Lost Reality

(Volume 1)

Bobby Simonds

ISBN: **9798814528216**

ISBN 13: **XXXX**

Library of Congress Control Number: **XXXXX**

LCCN Imprint Name: **Independently published**

Front Cover & Editing by author.

https://bobbysimonds.com/

<u>**Contacts:**</u>

bobby.simonds@gmail.com

www.facebook.com/bobbyraysimonds

www.facebook.com/bobbyrsimonds

https://www.tiktok/@authorbobbysimonds1

I dedicate this series to Neil Lamb, Alyssa Leonard, and Kaitlyn Jones. I appreciate your kindness and friendship, and even relationships. Without realizing it, all three of you had a hand in the emotions I was able to carry while creating this magical book series!

Chapter 1

I won't let you down; you're quite special to me. You know who you are. The issue is, is that I think I want it more than you. The other issue is that you don't have your shit together. You said you want more, and I can't blame you for something you deserve. Furthermore, the years we've known each other, and of those years we somehow fell in love, quite unexpectedly.

Both being divorced, we live separate lives, losing opportunities that we should be dealing with together, while we could be growing together – thru love and support.

Losing myself without somebody I know I can trust, I've never met someone like you…You are – and were – my: everything. Without you, well my life feels empty, and quite meaningless. It's my fault. Or the world's…I'm not quite sure what happened, but it's unfair, to say the least.

I couldn't help myself; I was exploring the wilderness and found a staircase that led to nothing. I thought, *well if I took a chance, maybe there would be a photo-opportunity at the top…* Oh, there was, just not in this reality…

I reach the top, I turn around – while raising my camera…Just before I could take a picture, and I accidentally hit the video record button, and trip backwards. I assume my fall would hurt, as there was quite a bit of a fall from the top of the staircase…Only, I fell into a different reality, and I found myself out of the woods, quite literally.

The layout of the land was different than where I last was and the air and feeling was totally wrong. I was even wearing different clothes than just a few moments ago. I wasn't confused as I have heard of this occurring to people. It is said that a doppelganger (a person that looks like you, but is from a different reality, or dimension) slips thru your world, and you basically switch realities and/or lives (and visa verse). Everything they did, you are stuck with. Furthermore, your life is pretty much the same. Such as your career, your materialistic choices (car, house/apartment, money) and the people may be familiar to you, but all have different names and locations. This isn't something new, just something that has always been covered up by all governments throughout earth & time. The only thing that really is different from one reality to the next is perhaps the lay of the land, such as current events. Like for another example, we have just entered a new phase of electric automobiles and Artificial Intelligence, perhaps the next reality may be on a totally different timeline than ours, perhaps a new nuclear war, another Holocaust, or even a Jurassic era!

The sun is brighter, the air seems cleaner, and however, there seems to be something wrong, there aren't any people…

I begin walking down from where I stood, which seemed to be a small park, with no sounds of animals, humans, vehicles or anything. It's almost like I am the only person alive.

The first building I approach is an old movie theatre with posters in the window of some upcoming movies, with the year 3022, instead of 2022; so there's that!

There is defiantly a type of disturbance in the atmosphere compared to my previous life. Only, I still don't see any people, along with only a handful of vehicles left on the street. It's quite similar to those towns we would see on a historical documentary about *fake towns* for the nuclear test sites. At least there were manikins in the windows and standing on the sidewalks…There aren't even birds chirping…

I attempt to peer in the window at the front ticket booth; but to no avail do I see anything, it's painted black, and it seems like another failed attempt to seek out any signs of life.

Just aside from the theatre, is a small enclosed book station, with literally, one remaining book? I lift the lid, reach in, and pull out the only book.

To my surprise, the book feels brand-new. Even the pages are crisp, almost as though it was just delivered right off the press!

Aside from the brand-new appearance, the title of the book is titled: *Everything has changed!*

Before I decide to read it, I think I should continue walking and seek out anyone, in existence.

What seemed like hours in time was only a mere twenty minutes. I came to the edge of the main road, and still haven't come across any sign of life. There aren't any homes at the end of the main road, so I decide to see if any of the remaining vehicles parked along the street work; let alone, have any keys in them.

Within a few minutes of attempting to get a car door open, I sit in the car and found a push-start button. The engine turns over,

and shows that there is 900 miles left before

the car runs out of battery. Luckily they still

have steering wheels and a gear shift, not

much has changed in all reality…

Chapter 2

After driving about 100 miles, the sun set, and I decided to pull off to the side of the road and read the book I came across. I am super hungry, but couldn't find any food, luckily, however, there were unopened bottles of water inside the trunk of the car, and so that was a plus.

I leaned the back of the chair back as far as it could go, and turn to page one.

The following is how it begins:

Blade

I feel as though being creative is a curse with love and compassion. Almost like you have no choice, but it was really never yours to decide.

Meaning you choose love, but you become part of the lost sheep; wasting what precious time you could have once offering to the world something from your creative talents. On the other hand, if you choose the creative path, you then become cursed with love, going from friend to friend, lover to lover, spouse to spouse – and so on. Only to feel suffocated, since you feel enslaved, no matter what you do.

It sounds terrible, but there are few who live happily ever after - in our line of work; and quite often, it's *smile for the camera* – and hate each other at home, and be that fake couple for the American audience, only to lead the masses into a trap – called marriage, with the one that you never truly loved.

Blaze

I know it's hard because society pushes a lot on you. Even more if you are in the spotlight!

Blade

And then you have your family who is supposed to have your back, but only with what they want for you to achieve for them; while they can still manipulate you. Conversely, if you stay, and want it more, it's a dream that they are, themselves, influencing for you – revealing what could be, then badmouthing you; almost like ripping your guts out from within – only to trash your dreams and potential abilities...

And from that influence, they deep-scar you for life, so when people like us make it big, we play nice for the audience, but are cold, cold-hearted people – because, from the actions and words around us, have scarred us badly, over time – forcing us to shut down like robots, and/or the puppets that we have become.

Then, "they" create scandals and we become victimized, we become so dead inside. All the while, I often wonder if it is even worth it…any of it….

But I am always reassuring myself by saying _yes_. ***Yes: it is all worth it***. This is why:

"For the reason that, other non-creative people, cannot understand it; they cannot wrap their humble, yet simple minds around such a concept. It isn't the awards; it's not the red carpet, the lavishness that goes along with it, the money, the freedom, or the celebrities that you meet. It isn't even getting all the clutter inside your mind that is haunting the creator from the stories…its way more than all of that. Our passion is our own

curse…"

Do you know what it all comes down to? That one person, that sticks with you, from time and time again; that one person…that you never expected.

Blaze

When you become a celebrity, everything changes; you don't have privacy, and everyone wants to be friends with you, no matter how dirty they did you, everyone wants a piece of that pie – and suddenly you have 30 cousins you didn't even know existed, friends that claim to be friends, and family members you distanced yourself from awhile back, all the while, they decide to let things go so they can mooch from you, and even take you for all what you once stood for, you comply because you didn't realize they were using you.

That one person, I met last week. That girl, that wouldn't be in my life if Covid-19 never came about: *The Universe clashes*.

Blade

There truly aren't words to express the odds from .0000000001% that we came together, Blaze.

Blaze

If we wouldn't have a Pandemic caused from COVID-19, I wouldn't have stopped acting and I never would have worked here!

If I was friends with Tammy; and I wouldn't have seen her Facebook post, and reached out about this job… If COVID wasn't a thing, we wouldn't even have this job… If it wasn't for COVID, I would've moved to California, in June; and it's nearly Christmas 2019!

Blade

If it wasn't for this job - our lives would be filled with more chaos, only without each other.

Blaze

I know. I cannot even imagine my life without you, after we clicked, upon my first day together. I'm thankful that you "claimed" me, to "train" me. I understand that it wasn't just because I was the hottest girl to enter the workplace. Now, it was because you worked solo for two months, and you felt a connection towards me, even before speaking with me.

What I know now, is that you are the missing piece in my complicated life. Without you, I wouldn't have learned to stand-up for myself like you have taught me to do. You are a huge influence in my life – and I seriously cannot fathom my future and/or my life without your presence.

Blade

Our souls felt lost and shattered; our dreams felt like failures and a bunch of **_what ifs_**; what if we didn't have the Pandemic…We wouldn't have just come up with the best story of friendship. So, THANK YOU COVID. I BOW TO YOUR EXISTENCE, BECAUSE I MET MY BESTFRIEND, all thanks to you.

Blaze

I am so happy to have a best friend like you; I thought I had friends, until you came along. _**YOU**_... **_You showed me what a true friend is: loyalty, love, companionship, passion, respect, and even entertainment, a shoulder to cry on – and surprisingly: HUGS!_** I can honestly say that you are my true, best friend; and one that I have no _sexual_ experiences with, because you've shown me, that we can be friends – without fucking! Maybe someday, but not currently!

Blade

Thank you – I think? Even so, you are not getting me to cry, I realize you must follow your passions, which you can only carry-out in California. Being in New York sucks, but I will find myself there, one day sooner, rather than later.

So, I say thank you, ***TO YOU***, <u>**Blaze**</u>, for taking a chance to listen, laugh and cry with me, only to trust me… You are more heart than any – one person: a pure soul; and I love you for that, in the friendliest way possible. Nothing more, and nothing less than my best friend; which I met from surviving COVID, with you.

Blaze

Battling COVID and anti-maskers, we must be superheroes! Except neither of us could be a side-kick; we just complete each other's' super power!

Blade

All protected by the powers of the universe.

Electricity, pure energy and love, is our main source

of superpower, because nobody has it, quite like us.

Blaze

EXACTLY!

Blade

They have fainted sparks, we have merging bolts! This makes our superhuman, and superhero power stronger than any, one-person on the planet, including the entirety of the universe.

Blaze

Now let's get this party started, and kick the doors into Hollywood, where we will bring the lightning, the wind, the energy, all who stand there on the sidelines, with their mouths dropped to the floor, all because they were, **_speechless_** by pure, passionate souls!

Well, I gotta say, that was a different

opening to a book! I decide to continue

reading, seeming how I won't be able to

sleep anytime soon. You know, after I

became interested in this book!

The Journal:

Chapter 1

Standing in a hallway, I couldn't help but notice how incredible quiet it is. It was eerie, sure, but it was almost disturbing – with how noiseless it is.

A few moments of short thoughts with trying to ignore the 'sound of silence', I began hearing grunting noises; it isn't a machine, however, it almost sounds as though it is the sound of disturbed animals. Not one or two, per say, but millions with the sound transference mainly on them; almost as though the noise from these bloodthirsty bounces off from the ground and the atmosphere simultaneously; forcing your ears to only focus on the grunting and growling protruding from these disconcerting creatures…

As I stood, I leaned against the open-doorway, not realizing I was no longer standing in a hallway. I now find myself in the middle of a roadway, in the desert, on the ground; since I fell from what I thought I was clearly - not leaning against the doorframe, but, moreover, open air!

The sky grew dark as the flying zombies rushed closer to my location; I jump in my vehicle, and hope and pray that this won't be my demise!

The sky curtained from soon-to-be destruction, then my mind 'clicks.' What I am hearing are winged creatures; only they are non-existent species – on earth. Then I see what is protruding toward me from the blackness: FLYING ZOMBIES!

As they swarm inward, I hunch down in a defensive position, then I close my eyes and count to ten – suddenly, all becomes calm and at peace, I awoke; it was merely a horrific nightmare! It felt very vivid, almost as though it were a vision from the near future…strange!

As I lay in bed, I couldn't help but lay in under my warm comforter, and then I realize, I'm not in my bed, but in the spare bedroom at Blaze's house.

Blaze swings the door ajar, and then jumps next to me on the bed. Our eyes meet, and we both smile, without saying anything at first…

Blaze spent much of the day cleaning and throwing away the last-minute items, just before saying farewell to her apartment. All of her furniture sold, except for the last mattress – which she didn't care about.

I lay comfortably on her bed while watching her clean. I didn't have anything more to do, except keeping her company. I watched her vacuum, then sweep, as she finalizes her duties with mopping. It was strange to see, because it's out of her norm!

Living in a Pandemic is filled with new adaptions, struggles, and barriers.

Including the media implementing daily fears!

Night sets in, and Blaze decides to shower after sweating all day from cleaning – which she finally is satisfied upon… I lay on her mattress in the living room; then I hear the water switch off, as I could hear Blaze pulling the shower curtain back, to step out and dry off.

"We should go out, Blade. It's been a long day, I'm tired. However, it is my last day here, with you. I want to make you happy." Blaze's voice echoes throughout the apartment, bouncing off the empty walls.

"Yeah, we should. Ironically, I already assumed that we would." I respond.

Suddenly, Blaze stands in a yellow towel in the entry way of the living room. The water from her hair slowly dripping from being wet and the aroma of her personal cleaning products fills my nostrils. Now, I wish I didn't wear sweatpants, because seeing my hot, Viking friend standing in nothing but a towel, forces my hormones to rise – along with my dick!

"I suddenly find myself standing awkward here, Blade!" Blaze expresses while laughing; as her eyes lock with my boner.

I laugh it off then respond, "*Olive Garden* sound good for dinner?"

"That sounds perfect, actually. You sure do like Italian food, don't you?" Blaze responds.

"Well, I'd prefer Mexican, but you don't like spicy things, and I've really got to be in the mood for seafood, which I am not." I explain.

"Okay, that's fine. Can you at least avert your eyes, so I can change?" Blaze expresses, while holding the flap in her towel.

I took a moment to respond, because I still had an erection, and I realize it isn't going down anytime soon. Ironically, I have seen Blaze nearly naked several times, and this is only the second time I put my guard down, by revealing my erection. I know she appreciates it, but I am still a guy, and she is quite an attraction.

"I am finding to look away quite difficult, and as we both know, you're leaving tomorrow, and I'm photographing you in my mind! I don't wanna forget you – or any part of you!"

I finally rose from the bed, as she slaps my inner thigh, forcing me to remove myself from the comforts of her mattress – all while forcing my boner down!

I decide to go outside and smoke, while she gets dressed. Before exiting her living room, I go to turn back and say something, but instead my mouth gapes with my tongue partially hanging loose, as she

drops her towel… I stumble backward, as

she turns her head to glance at my impartial

awkwardness. She laughs, shakes her booty,

and then farts. That was enough to get me

out of the room in a hurry!

Chapter 2

The White House changes the status from Pandemic to Epidemic – which means it's not as wide spread, and is more or less concentrated in various regions. This basically comes down to where the most population is, and how many are being restricted from leaving their cities, to spread the virus.

It's been months since Blaze had made her move, and the government is now in the midst of a 5th stimulus package – $2,000 per month, until the siege is over;

which they claim will be by Christmas of 2024. What this basically means for me, I will be financially set to leave – as planned – by the end of Christmas!

I begin to pack all of what I currently own and care about into the trunk in my car, then laid a blanket over top; then I close the latch to my car.

The house, congress and the president came to an agreement by allowing the last stimulus relief package, with two thousand dollars, as a once a month, direct payments; following unemployment at $2800 per month, until the end of the Pandemic –

December 29th, 2024; giving me at nearly

$4,000 in unemployment benefits allowing

me more than financially prepared!

Checking my available balance, I was

flabbergasted with the back-dated payments

with the once a month payments of the

$2,000. To my dismay, they back-dated it

from April of 2020, giving me a year and a

half's worth of back pay; equaling $42,000.

Since my current vehicle is falling

apart, and I highly doubt that the car will

even make it 1500 miles, I decided to rush to

the local Mitsubishi dealership, and see what I can purchase.

I was split between three vehicles, with all three being under $20,000. The first one was used, but sporty, an Outlander Sport with 4x4-option. The second, the same thing, but brand-new, with only ten thousand miles, and the 3rd option, an all-new Mirage hatchback; which I decided to get, based on the gas mileage being up to 45 m.p.g.!

The car is cute, but not at all what I am used to, and not everything fit in the car, so I sorted thru my shit, and thru majority of it out!

While I transferred my crap from one car to the new one, I heard that grunting and growling noises from my dream. I slam the trunk down as fast as possible, and started my car. Before long, I saw the flying zombies from exactly one night before, within my nightmare. I slam my foot down on the gas pedal and took off like dude who just stole a car!

Then, to make things more complex, the hundreds of millions of people who took the booster shots (not the first two shots, thankfully, but the 3rd shot) for the vaccines to fight Covid-19, are turning ill, dying, and then returning as full-fledged flying zombies!

I turn the radio on, listening to any updates from what I don't already know. I flip thru the stations that continue to play music, and finally come across an independent news channel, that introduces a scientist.

Thus far, zombies cannot enter any kind of body of water – such as ponds,

streams/rivers/creeks/cricks, lakes,
including oceans. Furthering their
weakness with water, it has been noted by
newscasters that both rain and snow kills
them off, which obviously means, everyone
will flee to more tropical or northern,
mountain regions!

After turning the radio off, I receive a call from Blaze, which she expresses that meet in Texas, as it is the half-way point from my drive to meet up with her. Which I thought was awesome, since we're both about a days' drive away. Although, she may beat me there, since she has just recently purchased a Dodge Challenger R/T; however, I won't have to stop as often for gasoline stops!

We spent many hours on the phone speaking to one another, as we always had, prior.

In any regard, I was doing about 90 miles per hour, in and of traffic, fleeing from State Police, because they hadn't caught on with *Phase 4 of the Pandemic*!

I just cannot believe that this is based on this reality, let alone any reality!

It makes me wonder how life would be once all the humans that aren't sick will be once they reach tropical areas, and/or the mountains. If you consider the heard of humans fleeing and all fleeing to safety, just consider just a fraction of the population, there's not going to be enough room to settle in either area, as far as a roof over their heads; or even, food for that matter! Isn't that just typical for the media to push an agenda upon the population? If the zombies don't get em', then the humans will kill

other humans…too typical!

Okay, enough of my thoughts, let's

get back to the book at hand!

Chapter 3

We decided to try fleeing to Montana. It has everything we need there: nature, hunting, fishing, and no zombies! We don't understand much about the flying scorpions as of yet, but I am certain that they will have their fair share of weaknesses also.

As we enter Montana, I found a dinky motel that I pull the car into. I park just aside from the office, get a corner room on the first floor, and get back into the car. Blaze just waking up, she leans forward observing the shit-hole motel; and then responds, "Really?" I laugh, and park the car in front of our room.

Just before shutting the trunk, Buddy runs off and into the first patch of woods just aside from the motel. I give chase, calling after him, as Blaze takes her dog on the leash like a smart person would do.

I finally found him, and as I grab him, my shoe slips on the mud that met the wet grass, and I fell backward.

"Blade - NO!" Blaze screams in shock.

The last thing I recall is my head landing on the nearby rock, and closing my eyes.

Chapter 4

This morning; I felt today is just one of those days we all feel like, *Today will hold greatest conclusion – we'll all be shredded and eaten by zombies…Nope, cannot think like that; today will be great! Blaze & I will survive, because <u>we're</u> survivors!*

I roll over and found a beautiful, tall blonde woman lying in my bed; only, I don't recall falling asleep with anyone.

Quietly, I get out of bed, pull my jeans up, throw a pair of nearby socks on my feet, including my shoes; and even my wrinkled shirt that lay next to the bed.

I stood and sought a chair nearby, attempting to recall any memories from the previous evening: nothing.

As I sat, I observe the room, including this goddess that lay nude in the bed.

My head feels foggy, as I rub the back of my head, and pull my hand back, and found dried blood, from off my hand, which obviously came off the back of my hand. I ask myself, *what happened last night? It's all fogged memories…*

As she flips herself over to lie on her chest, the blanket escapes her, revealing her entire backside and her soft, pale buttocks. Immediately, I notice her tattoos that imprint both cheeks: her left, a Leprechaun. Her right: a pot of gold – only, instead of gold coins, it is gold cocks!

With one knee up, the blanket barely stays upon her. This now, reveals her sexy, pink, soft, and smooth, taco.

Suddenly, I hear a knock, which ultimately, sounds as though, it came from the front door. I pretend not to hear the sudden disturbance, even though the sound persists. Furthermore, the sound becomes more of a banging noise, almost as though, something heavy is slamming against the door – instead of a human hand. Moreover, it sounds as if, it is multiple objects creating the sound, rather than the original: one knock.

As the banging persists, I no longer can ignore the disturbance; I have succumbed to my senses and left the room to investigate.

I navigate toward the front entry, and find a window nearby. I pull back the curtain and take a gander outside. To my surprise, there are three human bodies, only they are zombies. Their shoulders are banging against the door, which sounds like a tree at this point. Meanwhile, they concurrently bump into one another, continuing to bang against the front door, as they swing themselves in a circular motion. I decide to dead-bolt the lock, and return to the bedroom.

To my surprise, the dogs are being too quiet; perhaps, they must be in total fear for what is opposite of the door…

As I step inward, the blonde lay still, with her eyes open, which now glaze upon me, just after re-entry?

I took the chair and then move it in front of the bed, and sit. Our eyes meet with our breathing calm and steady; becoming relentless, then heavy.

Suddenly, she slowly pulls back the blanket and begins to finger herself. Her eyes still locking mine, while biting her lower lip, caressing her breasts with her right hand; all the while, fingering her twat with her left.

The harder she bites down on her lip, the harder she squeezes her nipple and finger-bangs herself. It doesn't appear that she wants me to join her, only she seems that she is getting herself off with me observing her. Therefore, I simply stay put, while teasing her with my eyes, and my appearance. My shirt unbuttoned just enough to reveal my chest hair, my hair slicked back, and my legs open, with my arms crossed.

As she begins to orgasm, my memories simultaneously return to me, revealing that this girl is no stranger, and I hit my head on a rock the previous evening, making my memories a bit foggy.

Once I realized that I was with Blaze, after all, and that this woman was no stranger, everything not only became clearer, but better. Now the zombies outside the motel room made sense, along with the noises in the sky from the flying scorpions. I honestly didn't know what our next move was, per say, however, I'm right where I want to be, with her. Suddenly, I had my first flash back from last night, just before hitting my head.

I pull her hair out from her face, while hugging her from behind. As I gently touch her face, my breathing deepens, becoming more heavily, as hers does, also. I then kiss the side of her neck, just under her right earlobe.

"What are you doing?" She asks.

"Experimenting, while proving my love and affection, my love," I respond.

Even though she questions my motives; her face begins to glow from receiving just the right amount of affection.

Summer swings around slowly, redirecting me; just as our souls rekindle through our eyes, I press my lips against hers; and then the world around us vanishes, almost as though time had ceased altogether.

Through our first kiss, our feelings grew deeper, now more than ever before. With all of our doubts throughout our friendship, I took the leap of faith, and dove into the next step, proving to her (at last), that we are not just soul-bonds, but moreover, soulmates!

"I have ben fantasizing this very moment for over a year… It was worth the wait, with no regrets!" Summer responds happily, just as our lips retrieve from one another.

Chapter 5

I, at some point, had fallen back asleep, I do believe that falling on the rock the other night, I received a concussion, forcing me to feel drowsy, which also forces me to suddenly fall in and out of a deep sleep…Which led to this freaky, yet disturbing dream I must share!

The Dream:

Kenny sits in front of me, naked & humiliated; his arms & legs strapped down, his mouth taped shut, tightly; with his fear overclocked, at full speed; he clearly cannot move; nor he cannot scream for help; all he could do is anticipate my next move.

As I pace back and forth in front of my victim; I finally gain interest with how to end his life, while stopping his victims' from more pain & suffering. His domestic violence will no longer ruin others.

I grab for my rusty hatchet, and jab his hanging testicles, which then fall to the floor, sliding forward, with blood escaping the skin. His screams are luckily muffled, and I strike down again with the same hatchet, leaving him dickless.

I then walk over to my tool box, and grab a pair of needle nose pliers, after dropping the hatchet in a drawer. Then, I return to Kenny and pull out all of his fingernails, one by one, then continue on with removing his toe nails. He shakes profusely, in total shock and agony, while bobbing the chair back & forth. He attempts to bob the chair over, but gravity fails, and I grin.

I toss the pliers back into my tool chest, and grab my newest machete. I return to my bleeding victim, and stand behind him, scraping the machete against his lower abdomen, leaving deep cuts, working upward, slicing both his nipples off. I then bring my arms up, with both hands on the handle, then I swipe down, chopping at the back of his neck: once, twice, then finishing with a third!

His head dangles from the last bit of strength holding on from his neck; with blood splattering like a fountain of blood; and then I step away, and look from the front, and I puke, when his eyes protrude from the sockets of his head!

Regaining myself subsequently from vomiting, I force myself to chop off all of his limbs, and then put them in several black garbage bags; leaving his torso for last, I had to place in my only suitcase, as it wouldn't fit inside a garbage bag, without ripping.

I loaded the bags into the back of my car, and off I went into the night towards the woods.

Once I arrived to the woods, I turn my car into the corner of the blackened park, and listened into the air, before taking out the trash, quite literally. Once I didn't hear any signs of human life, I emptied my trunk and dragged the bags, then emptied them, and then scattered his body parts all around the woods. I found an opening within a quarter mile, and decided it would be a great spot for the torso. I grab the suitcase, then a small gasoline tank, close my trunk, and

return to the opening in the woods. There
was a mild breeze, but nothing that won't
stop the fire from burning Kenny's torso. I
placed all the garbage bags on top of the
torso, and then I splashed gasoline on top of
it, finished my cigarette, and tossed it down.
The fire roared all over, and I escaped,
before watching anymore, because the smell
was horrific.

I doubt it will be difficult searching
for my next victim. It won't be long, and I

will help another poor soul, move on from violence, inside his, or her, home.

Bearing in mind, tonight, the organization my best friend, Vanessa owns, is holding its weekly therapy session, for domestic abuse.

Vanessa nearly lost her life to a man she thought was "the one", only to find out in a few short months into her marriage, he was **not the one**, and was nothing more than a complete asshole, with a gnarly temper, and a horrific abuser!

Luckily, for Vanessa, I came into her life not long after her divorce, and was able to assist her as much as she did with me. I didn't realize it until after become friends with her, that I too, lived in a hostile marriage. I just was used to it, and didn't realize it wasn't normal. I knew we had our heated arguments, and lost the trust, friendship, and love years ago, I just didn't really take that extra leap to get out, until Vanessa came into my life.

Somewhere along our journey, however, after accomplishing our non-profit organization – for assisting domestic

violence abuse – I became vengeful.
Perhaps, it was listening in on the group
therapy sessions; with hearing the same
stories, which I felt the need to step in.
Whereas, with the police refuse to – both,
then and now.

Vanessa, as far as I am aware, has no
idea about this vengeance; as for her ex-
husband, has recently manipulated his way
back into her life, and is now dead and
scattered in the nearby forest. Surprisingly,
Vanessa is more distraught that he is
missing, than I would have concluded.

As I sit across from Vanessa outside at the local coffee shop, I attempt to reassure her for both her safety and well-being, to say the least.

Nearly ten minutes into listening and reassuring Vanessa, her phone rings. It was the lead, homicide detective. Detective Tom Charleston states that the police department in Faysville, Illinois (where we reside), discovered her dead husbands remains.

Vanessa stops crying, covers her hand, then her facial expressions change, drastically. Her fear escapes her, and she had this sort of, blank look of her 'thinking' cap on. After hanging her phone up with the officer, she springs out from her chair, rushes toward me, bumping the table with her hip – spilling the coffee all over the table – and hugs me from excitement. She then shouts out, "he is dead, Deagon is dead!"

Vanessa then whisks me out of my chair, and forces me to dance with her, twirling me around, while laughing, smiling, and shedding tears of relief.

As people grab a donut and a beverage, they then grab a chair that patterns a circle. It is a bigger crowd than past sessions; and I took it upon myself to bring out more folding chairs for the guests.

Once everyone stopped talking, Vanessa rose from her chair and introduced herself (as usual). Thereafter, a few women wanted to discuss the conflicting news about the discovery of Deagon; knowing it was her recently deceased husband – also knowing, he was abusive. While they bring up questions, they tread lightly, not knowing how Vanessa would handle an open discussion.

While Vanessa stayed content, she was more than grateful that she no longer has to live in total fear. She also doesn't have to ever feel her emotions with what he would or wouldn't do when he entered her premises, or be within three feet or more of her. She expresses the various emotional freedoms she felt - when she was first told the news - and she wasn't concerned one bit, with *the why* somebody would kill such a man, but instead, wish she could thank his *murderer*.

When the session ended, most people departed, however, there were a couple of stragglers taking their time with speaking to Vanessa, and hugging her as they were ready to depart.

One of the regulars came up to me, her name is Sally, and thanked me for doing God's work. I thought, *lady, you have no idea, and your welcome!*

I gave Sally a smile as she told me about how she wishes somebody would help with her abusive boyfriend, Matthew. "Matthew is a Christian name, and by golly, I'm telling you Brent, he is no true Christian. Matthew is a demon sent from

Hell, and he needs to be crucified." Sally expresses, while shaking her head, shedding a few lonely tears. Then she shakes my hand again, and then departs.

I assisted Vanessa with the clean-up, by putting away the chairs, dumping the remaining coffee in the sink, washing the pot, as she took care of disposing the coffee filter with the grounds in the waste basket. I sat the coffee pot on the towel to dry, upside down, and shut the lights off. Then we left.

Once I step into my home office, I moved the mouse cursor, and typed in Matthew Lyte in my search engine. I wanted to learn everything I could about this maniac, as I figured he is as good as any to add to my hit list.

The internet came up empty-handed with Matthew Lyte. I decide to go to bed, and do some in-person, research and stalking: where he works, what he looks like, how big he is, if he only beats woman, that sort of thing.

I turn my light off, after getting

comfortable in my bed, under my comforter.

Chapter 6

I must have hit my hard way harder than Blaze expressed to me about! That was some dream, and to be honest with you, it felt so damn real. Almost as though I lived thru the narrator's mind, saw what he saw, and I even woke with stomach pains from his vomiting fiasco!

My eyelids feeling heavy, I roll back over on the bed and slowly drift away, while holding Buddy, my warm dog.

"Tony, what the fuck is that behind the tree? Did you see it?" Max expresses wildly.

"Max, I think this is a good time to leave the woods!" Tony exclaims.

The two friends scurry to the edge of the woods, exiting before some strange creature causes any harm.

"Whew, that was close." Max spoke softly.

Max turns, but doesn't see his buddy. Suddenly Max hears his friend screaming as he never had heard before.

"Tony, where are you? Tony!" Max frantically searches nearby, but all he discovers is a large blood pool, with what he could only assume is Tony's left arm in amongst the blood.

Frantically, Max rushes to his car. In a panic he searches for his keys, unlocking the doors, and jumps inside – hoping that the car keeps him safe while dialing 911.

"This is 911, how may we assist your call today?"

"Yeah, you won't believe me, but some gnarly creature may have killed my friend. I couldn't find him after escaping the woods. And then, I went back in, after realizing he wasn't with me. I couldn't find him anywhere, where we last fled; but I did, however, come across a pool of blood, with what I could only assume is his left arm torn off his body. Send help, please!"

"Okay, sir. Where is your location? Please stay on the line, and keep calm, help is two minutes away."

Once the first responding officer arrived at Green Lakes State Park, New York, Max attempts his best to repeat his story. The police officer rolled his eyes, and then asks if Max was on any *illegal narcotics*. Frantically, Max couldn't keep calm, as he knew time was against him, if Tony had any chance of survival, if he wasn't dead already.

The officer followed Max into the woods tracking down the pool of blood, as the officer did discover the severed arm. Which of course, the officer grabs for his radio, and then requests back-up; plus a search and rescue team.

Within hours, hundreds of agents, both with the F.B.I., and Army, had appeared from both the ground and sky. The area was swarmed with onlookers and rescuers alike. Dusk soon became darkness, and searchlights lit the woods. I grew impatient knowing that Tony is most likely vanished forever; and the search team spans enough of the woods that they should have come across something by now. The lead investigator took my information and told me that I should leave, and wait for a call for more information.

Just as I was convinced to leave, screams could be heard in the distance following machine gun fire. I dove to the ground for cover, as bullets shot in all directions hitting more people than whatever is lurking deep in the woods.

As Max prays to his God, gunfire ceases to exist as the trees get pulled from the ground, and get thrown towards the ones shooting. A twenty-foot giant rises from the woods – which appears to be a human, but a giant – and begins fighting back. The bullets do nothing, but anger the beast more. Max escapes the area, only to never look back again.

"Sara. It's me, Rachael. I thought you said you were going to be ready to go for a hike by noon? You do realize it's

going on 4:30 already? Just because its

summer, doesn't mean we should go hiking

just as the sun sets!"

Rachael finally finishes putting her

boots on, rolls her eyes at her friend, and

locks the door behind her, only to enter into

Sara's new, Jeep Wrangler.

Arriving at a secluded part of the

woods in New Hartford, New York, both

girls assume that they have plenty of time

for cruising the trails and taking pictures –

both of themselves and nature alike…

"Blade, wake up, you're dreaming!"
Blaze expresses repeatedly while shaking
my arm. Meanwhile, Buddy tugs on my
lip, and I realize that was merely another
realistic dream. I then ask myself, *what*
the fuck is happening to me?

I finally force myself to take a shower, get dressed with the dirty clothing that I have, because I couldn't find my duffle bag, and leave the bathroom. Blaze waits impatiently on the bed, and looks up from me while holding both our dogs on both sides of her body.

"Feeling better Blade?" She

expresses. I nod my head in response, walk

toward the door, while stopping at the

curtain next to the front door. It appears that

the zombies have given up on us, for now.

Leashing both dogs, I open the door,

and step out, the dogs escape my grasp, and

Blaze bumps into me as I hesitate leaving.

Something feels off to me, and from her

bumping into me, I fall forward…

Landing hard on the ground, with

Blaze on top of me, we both push ourselves

off the ground – and me – and realize we left

our reality without our dogs and

belongings…

The adventure continues, stay tuned for

Volume 2, __The Blade & Blaze Story:__

__Escaping Hell__